Unit 5

Hudson

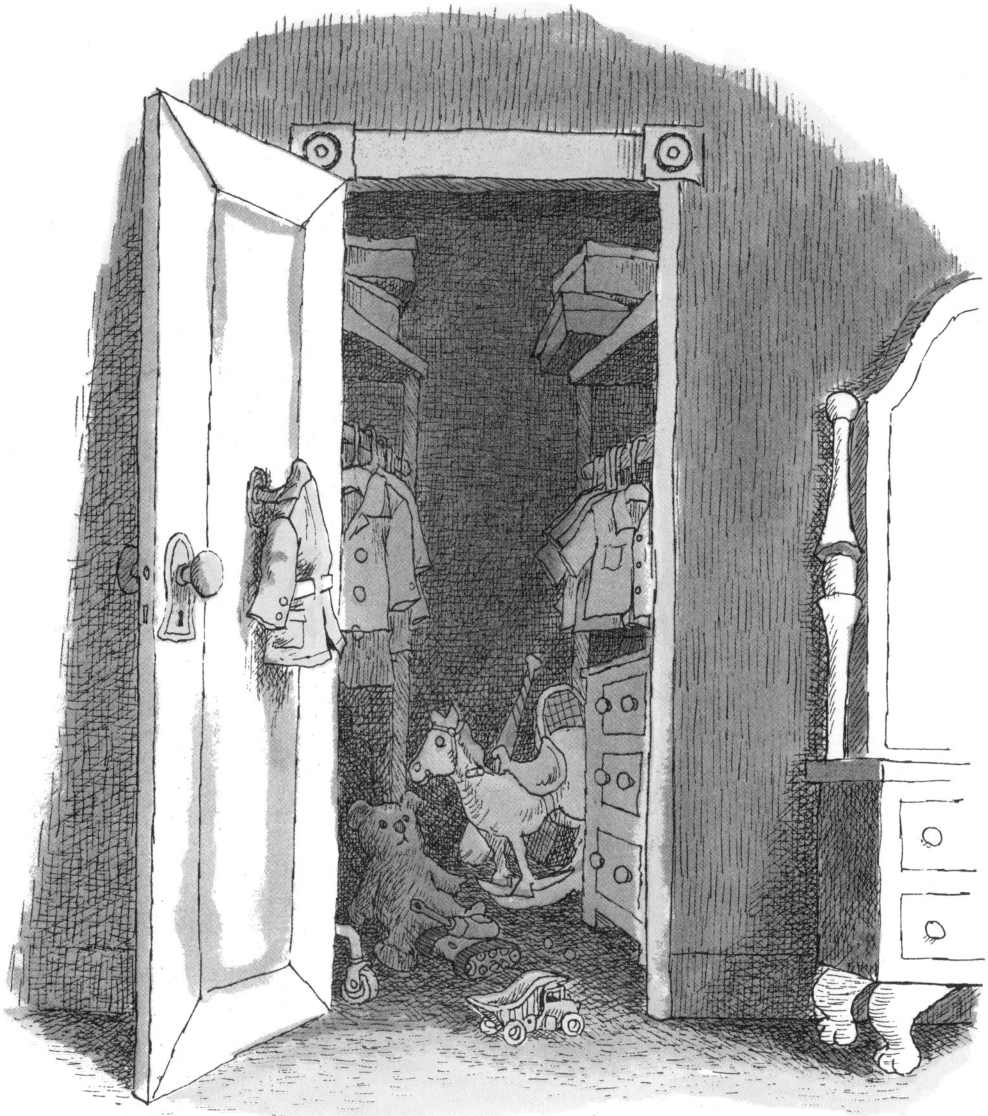

THERE'S A NIGHTMARE IN MY CLOSET

written and illustrated by Mercer Mayer

Dial Books for Young Readers
New York

a pied piper book

Copyright © 1968 by Mercer Mayer • Áll rights reserved
Library of Congress catalog card number: 68-15250 • First Pied Piper printing 1976
A Pied Piper Book is a registered trademark of Dial Books for Young Readers
A division of Penguin Books USA Inc.
® TM 1,163,686 and ® TM 1,054,312
Printed in the United States of America • C O B E • 25 24 23
THERE'S A NIGHTMARE IN MY CLOSET is published in a hardcover edition by
Dial Books for Young Readers • 375 Hudson Street • New York, New York 10014
ISBN 0-8037-8574-7

Marianna

From cotton to rabbit

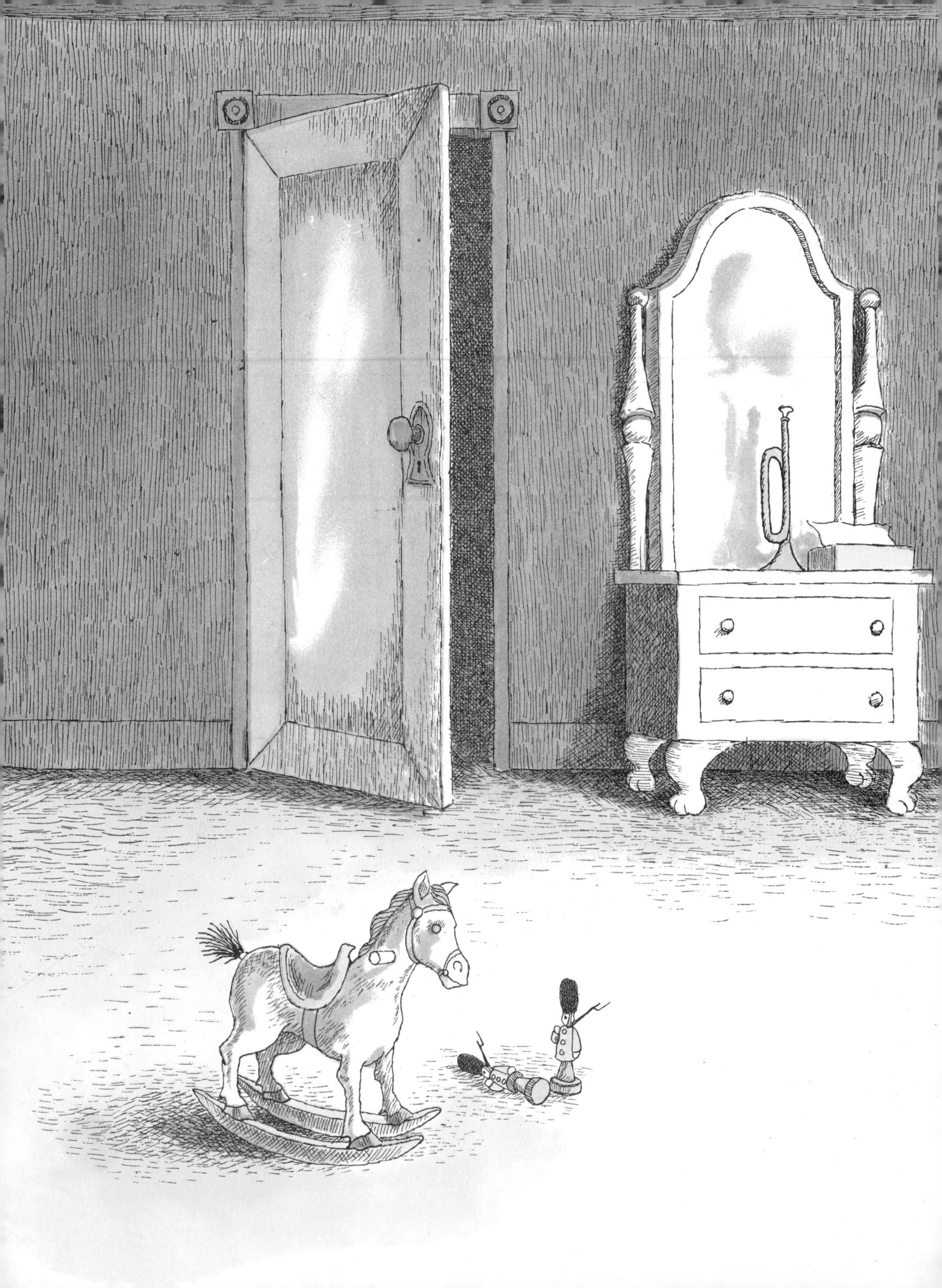

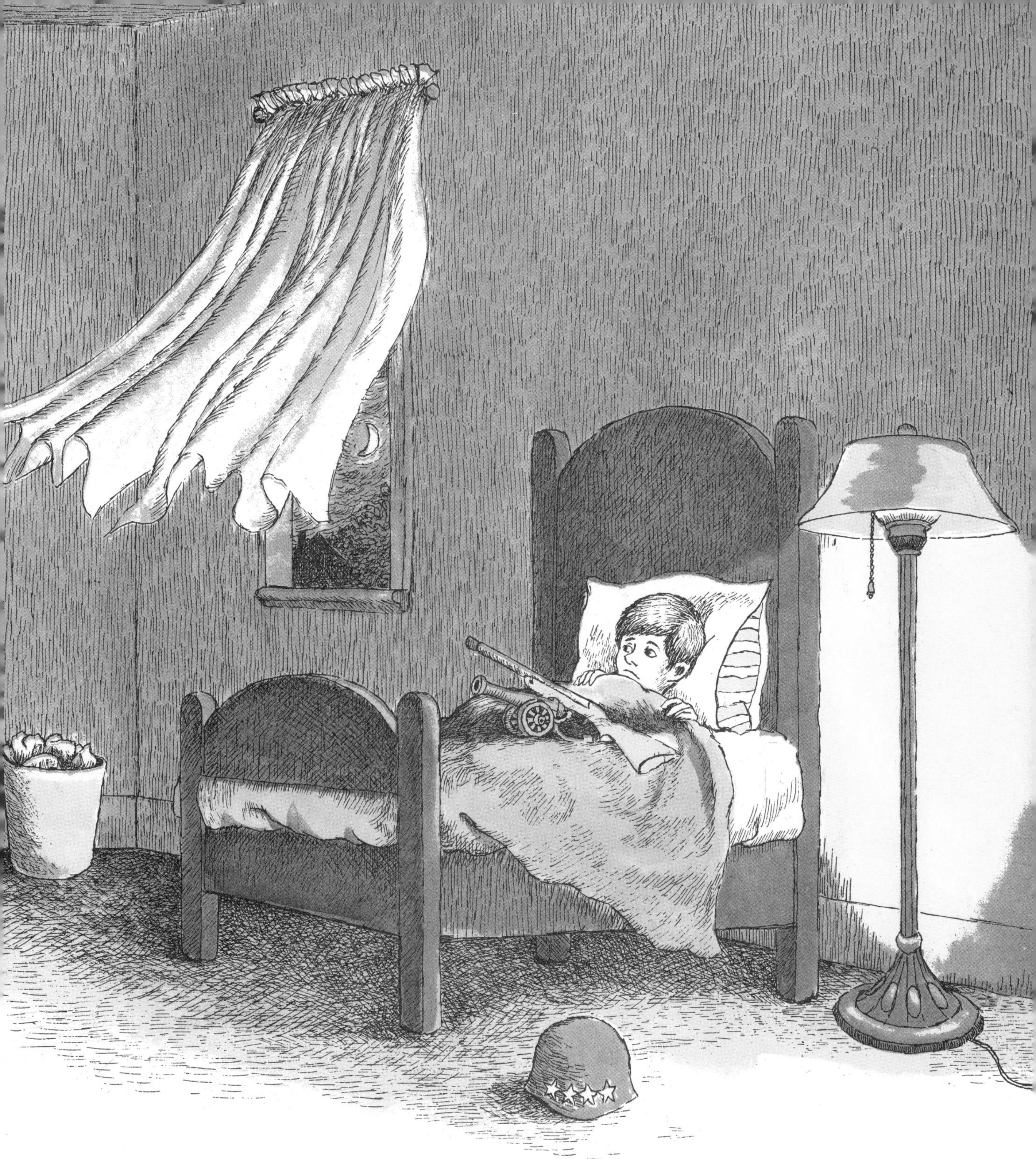

There used to be a nightmare in my closet.

Before going to sleep,

I always closed the closet door.

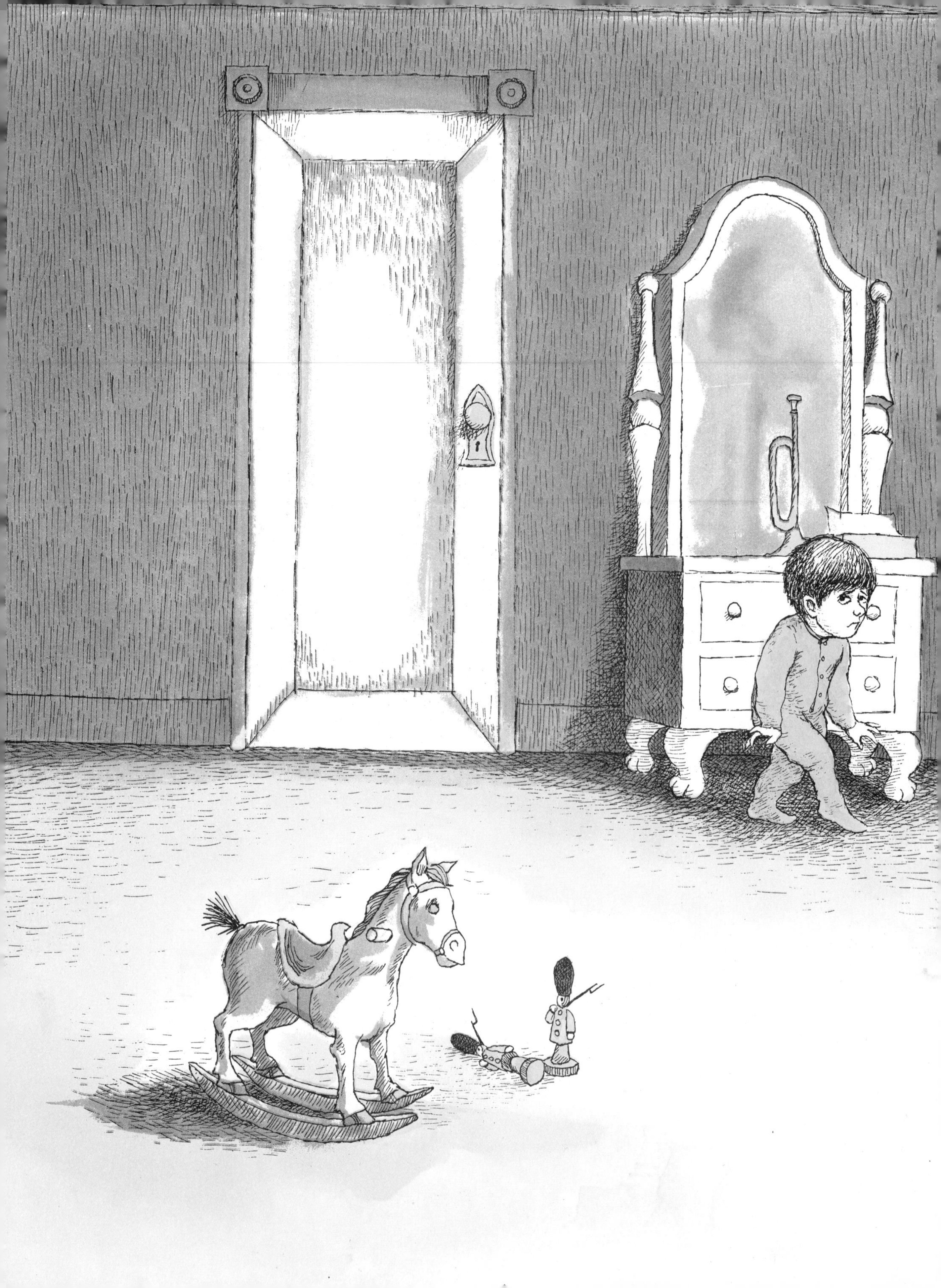

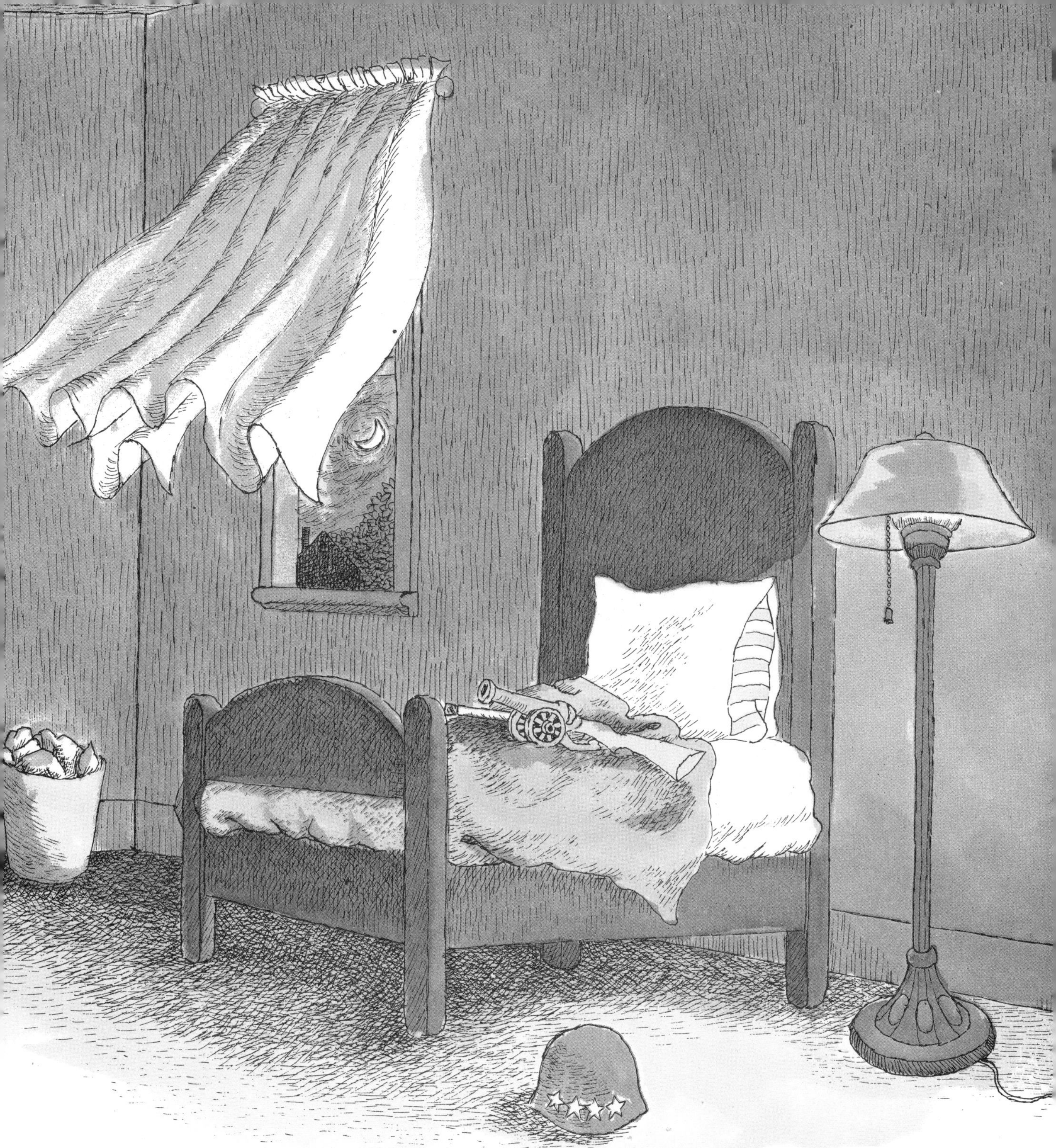

I was even afraid to turn around and look.

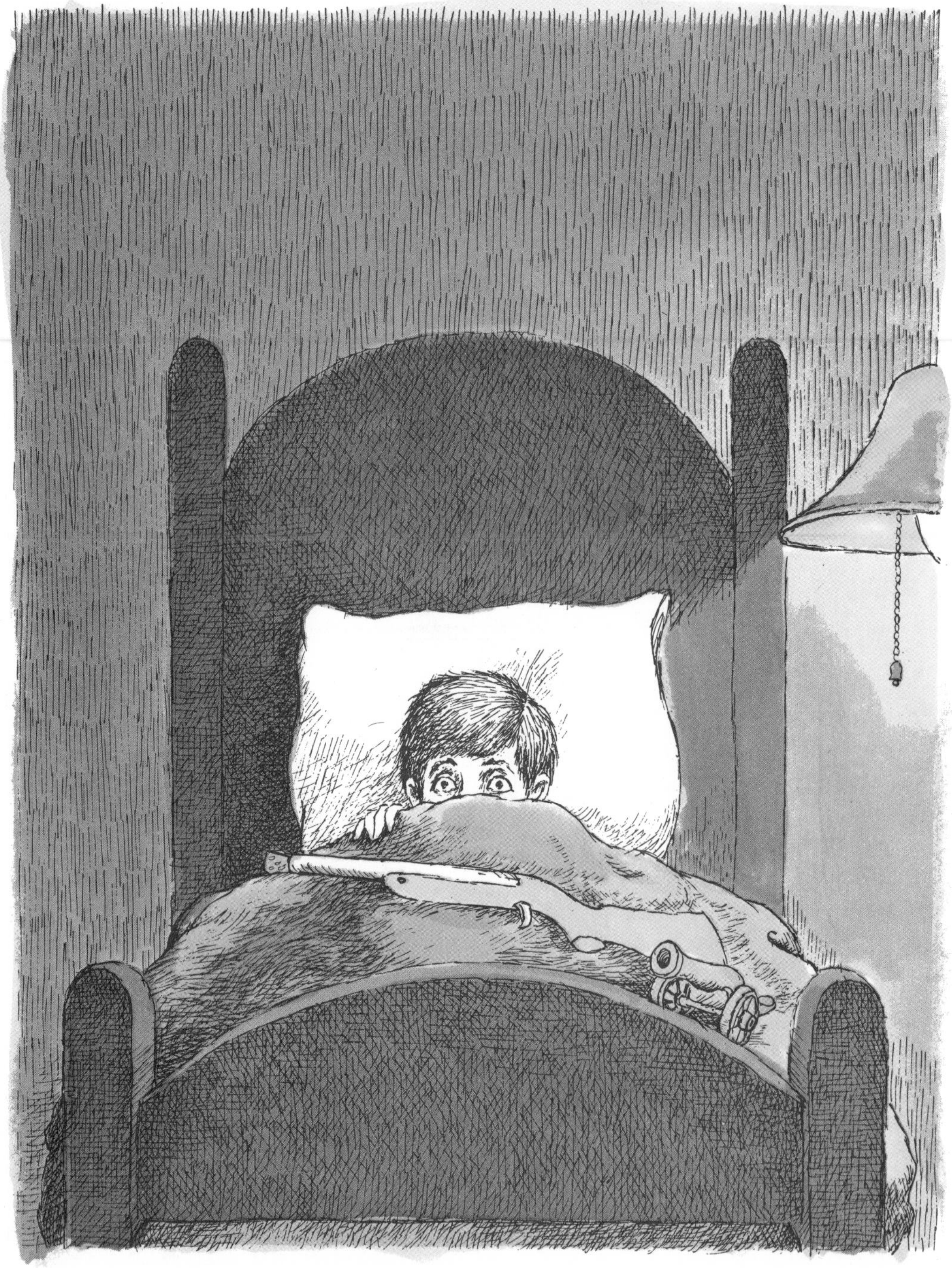

When I was safe in bed, I'd peek…

sometimes.

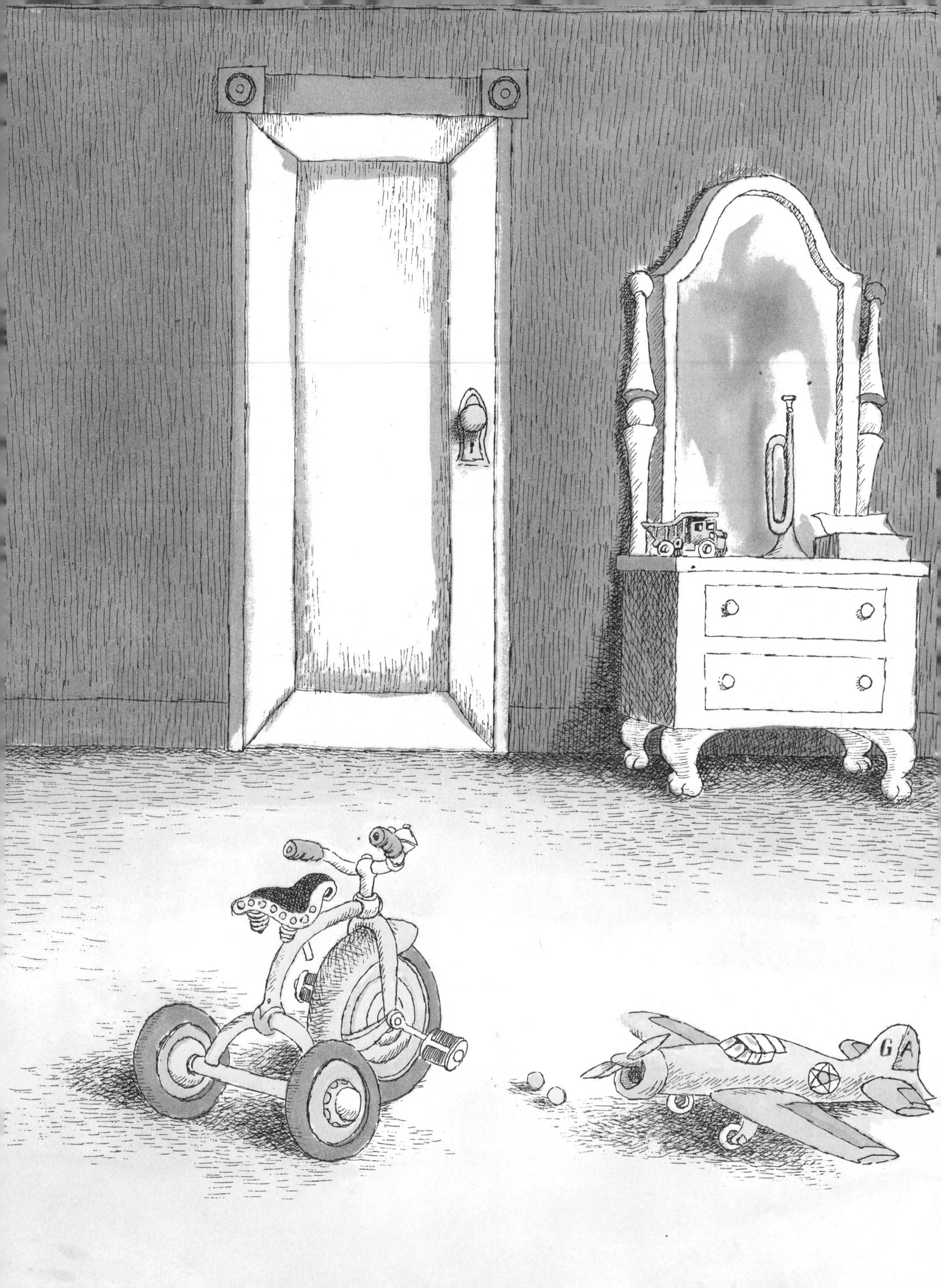
GA

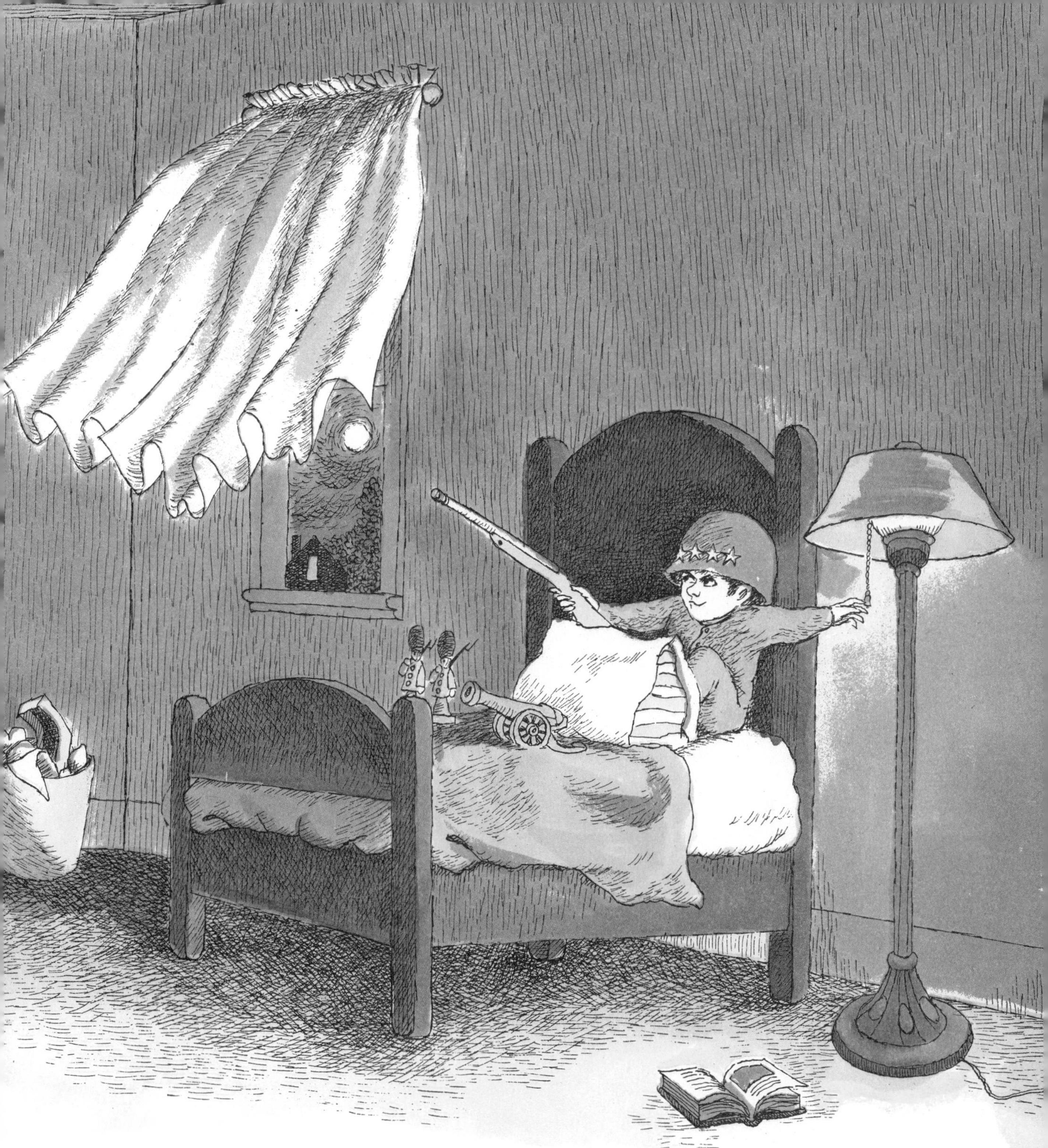

One night I decided to get rid of my nightmare once and for all.

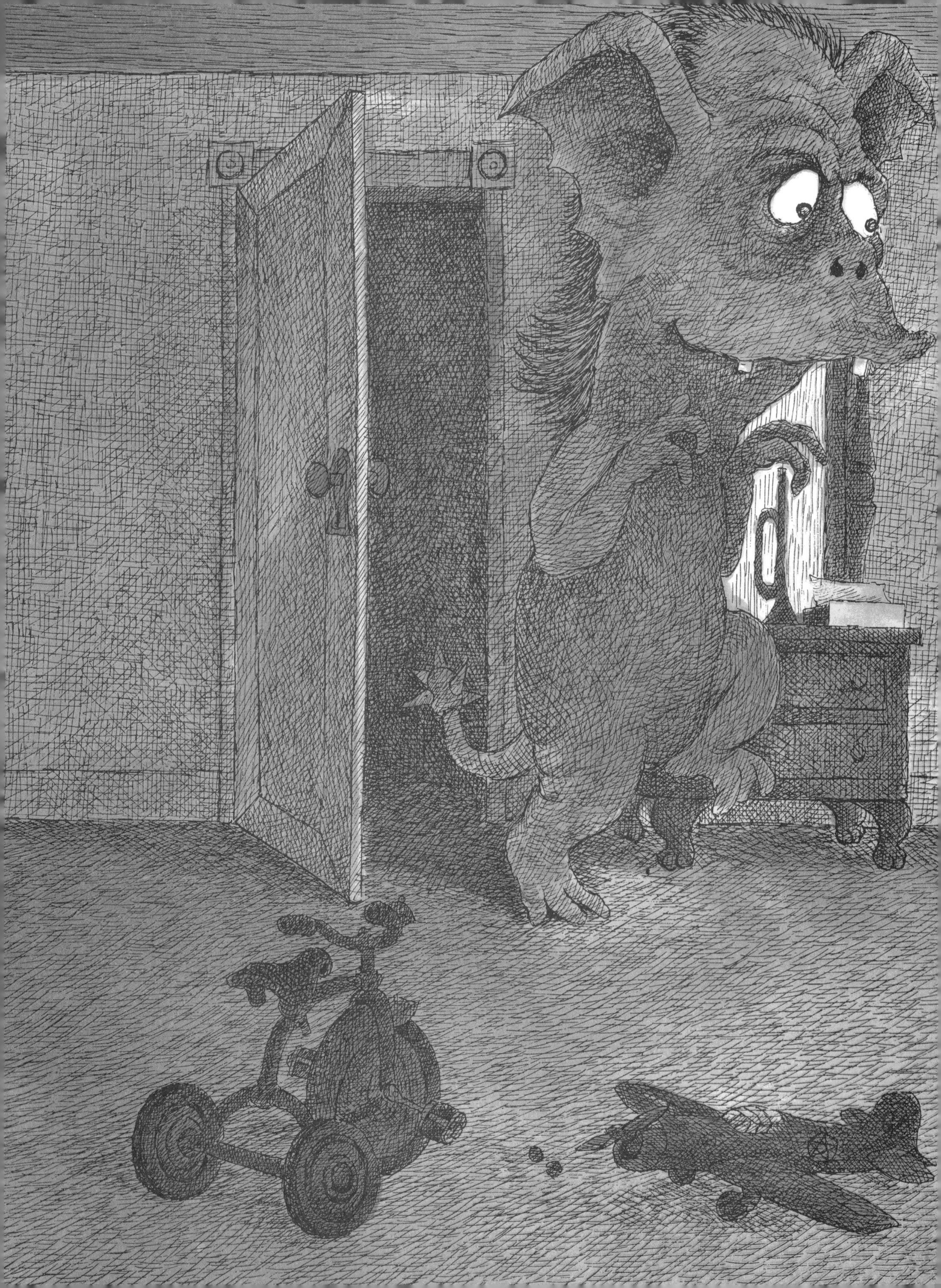

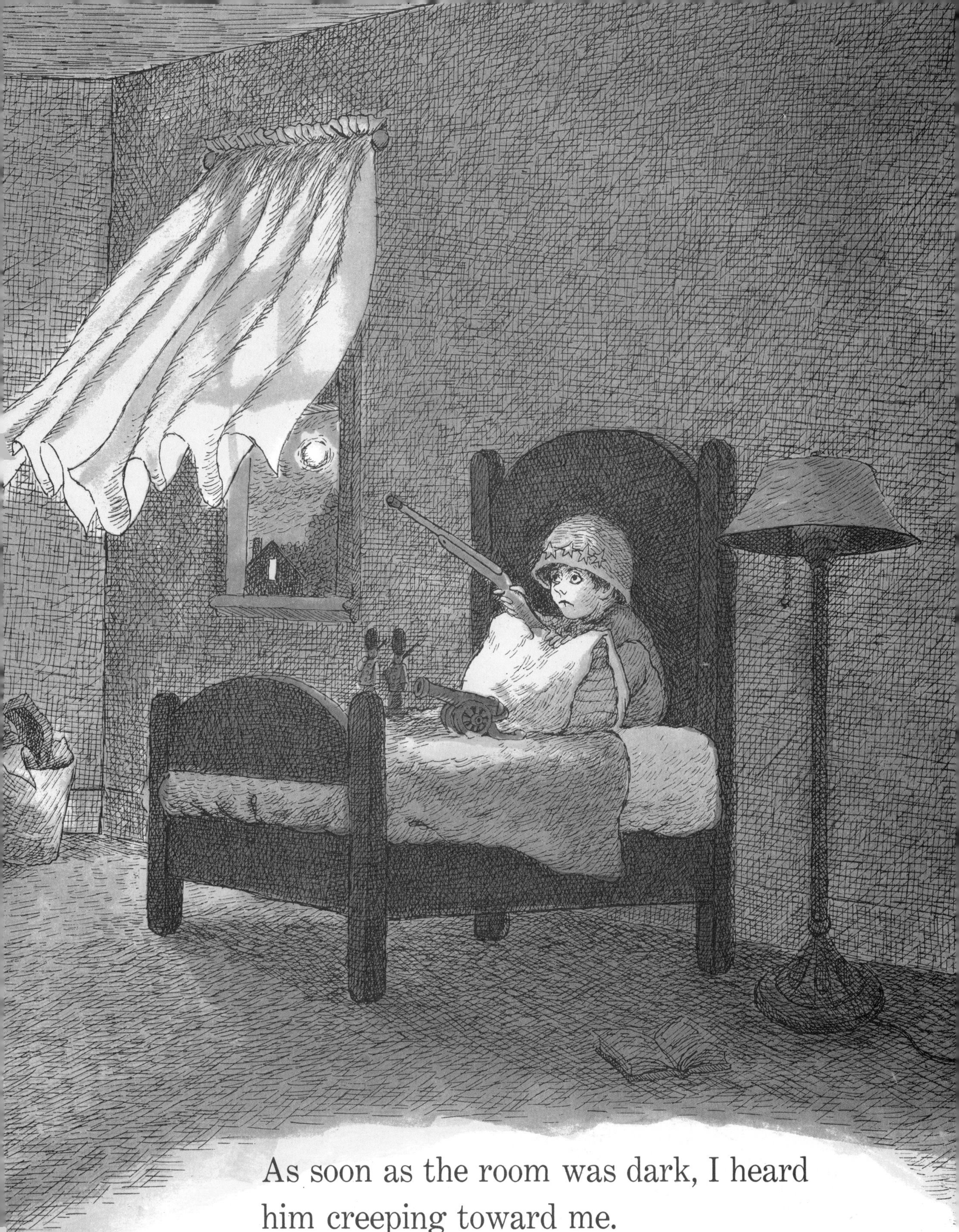

As soon as the room was dark, I heard
him creeping toward me.

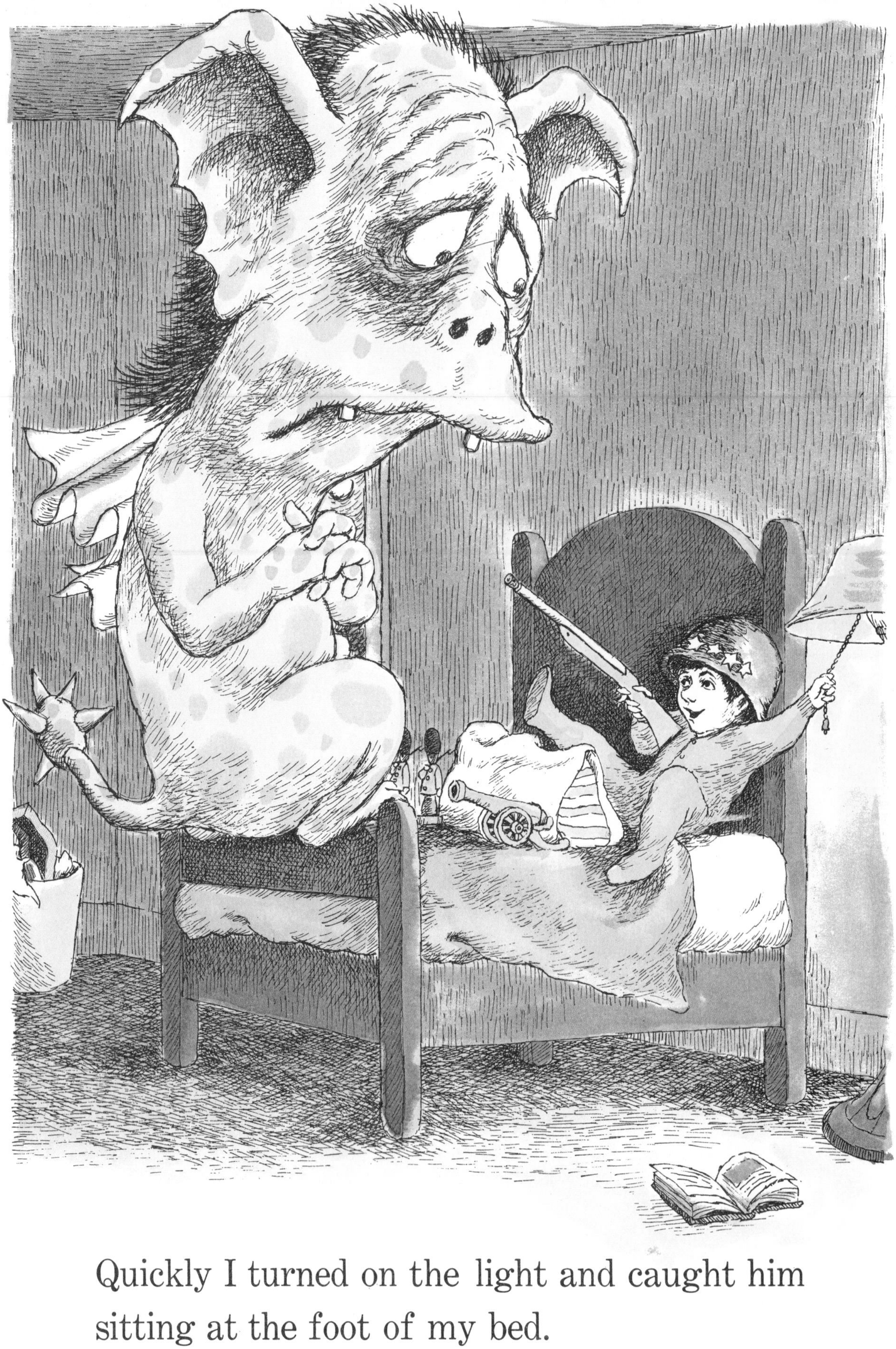

Quickly I turned on the light and caught him sitting at the foot of my bed.

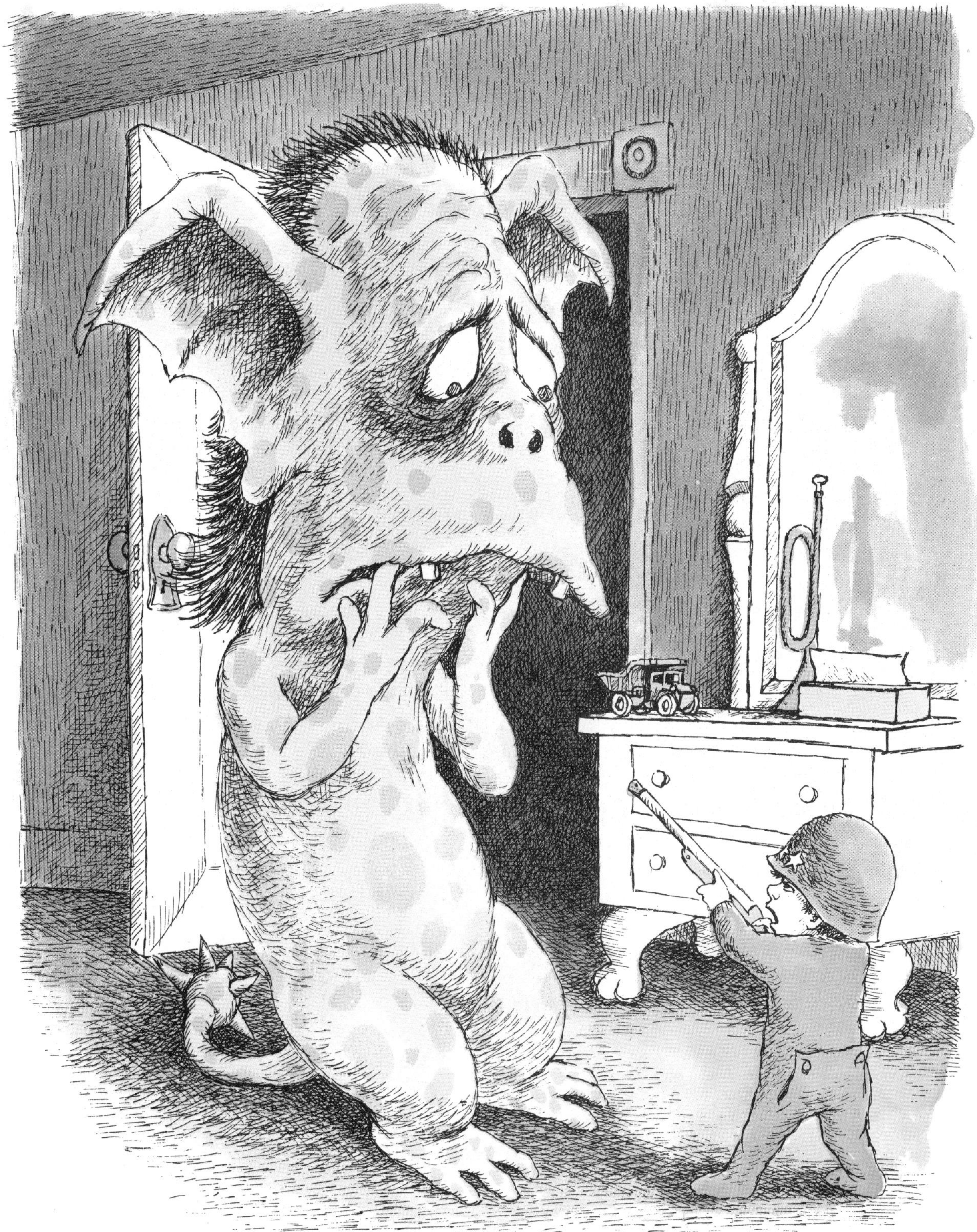

"Go away, Nightmare, or I'll shoot you," I said.

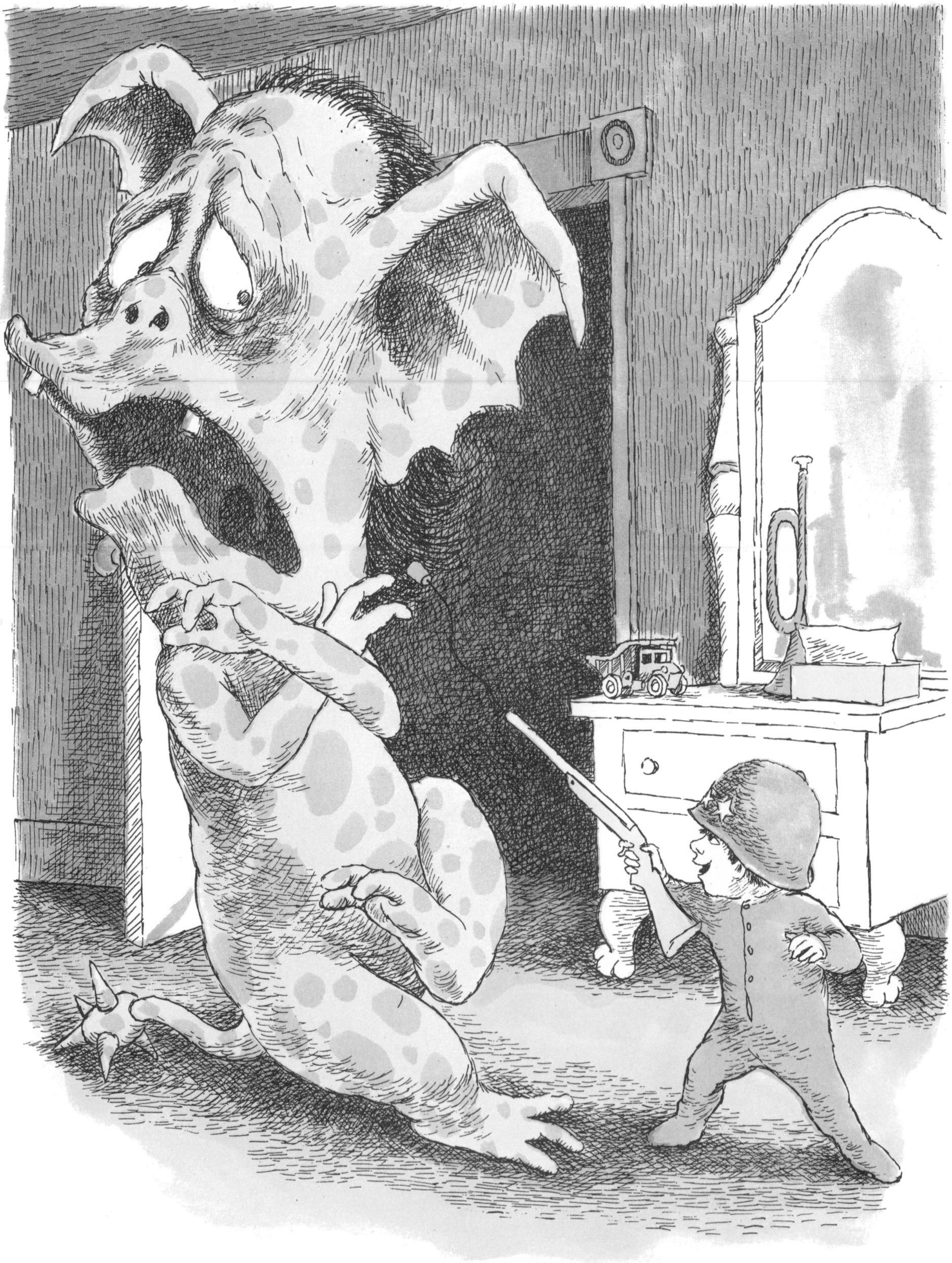

I shot him anyway.

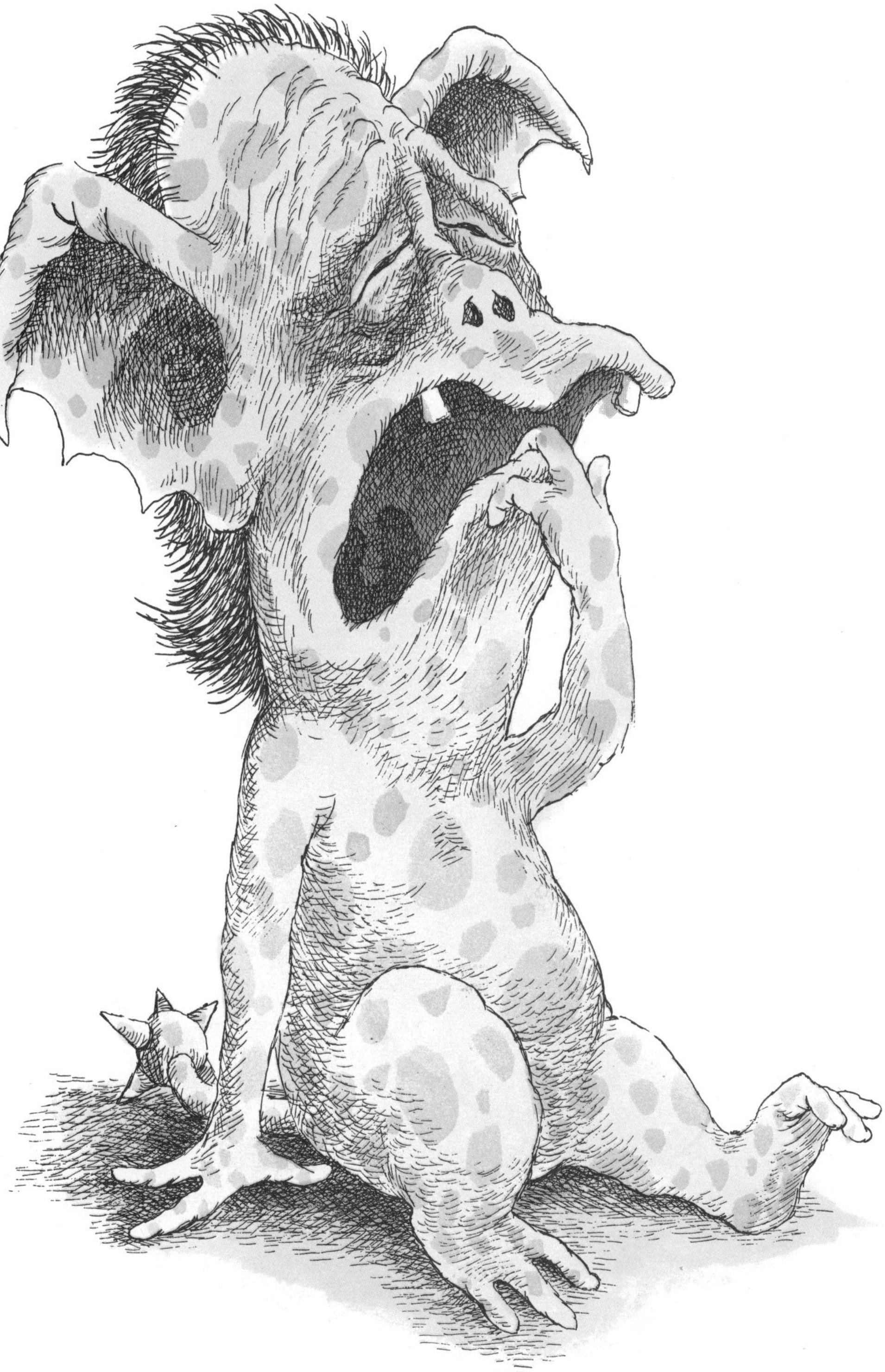

My nightmare began to cry.

I was mad...

but not too mad.

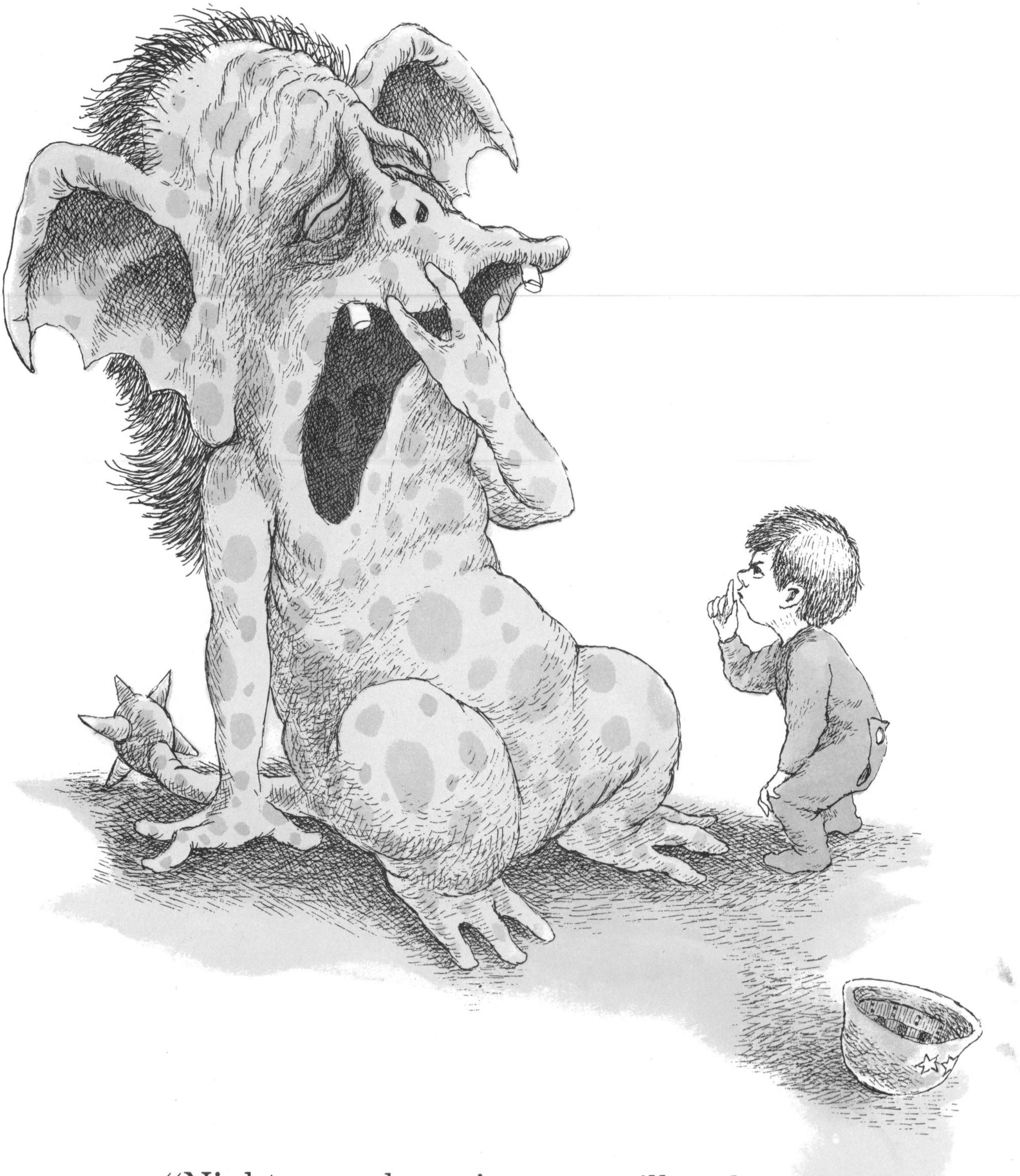

"Nightmare, be quiet or you'll wake
Mommy and Daddy," I said.

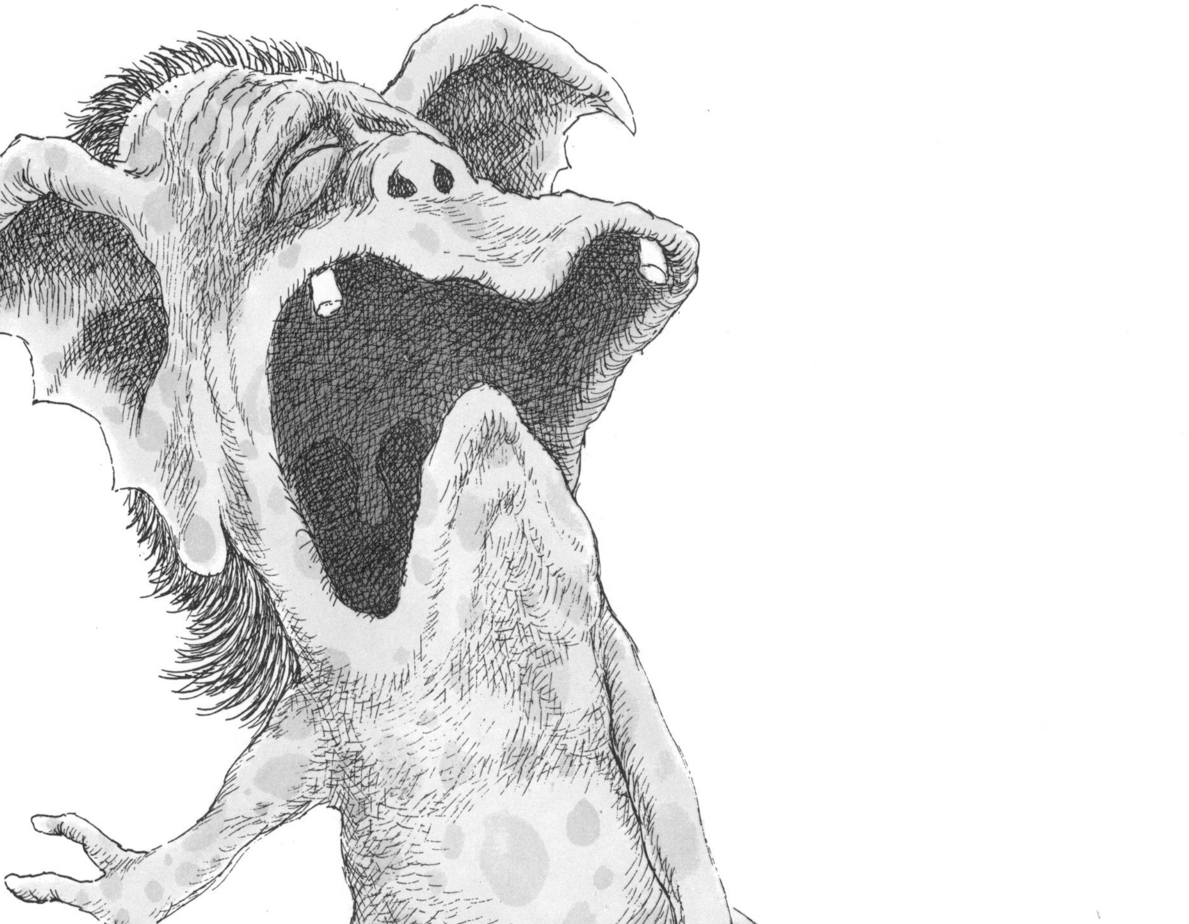

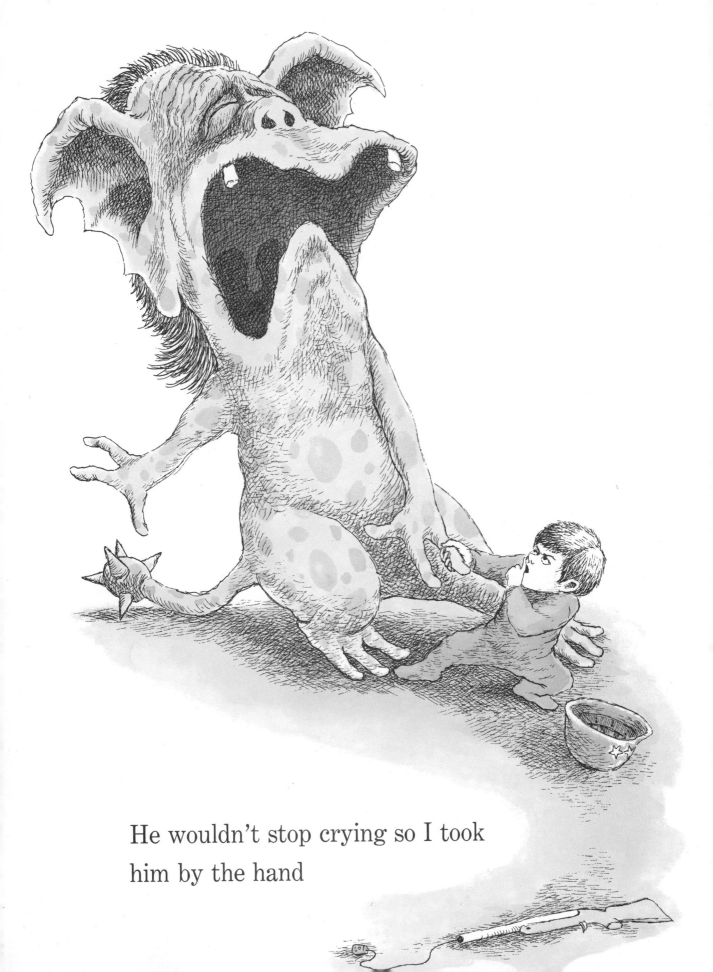

He wouldn't stop crying so I took
him by the hand

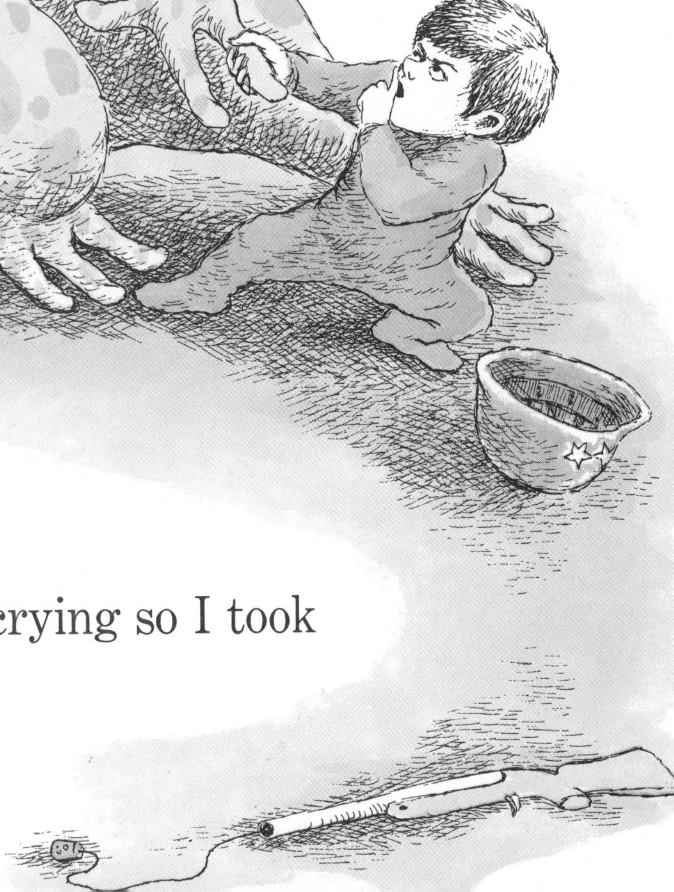

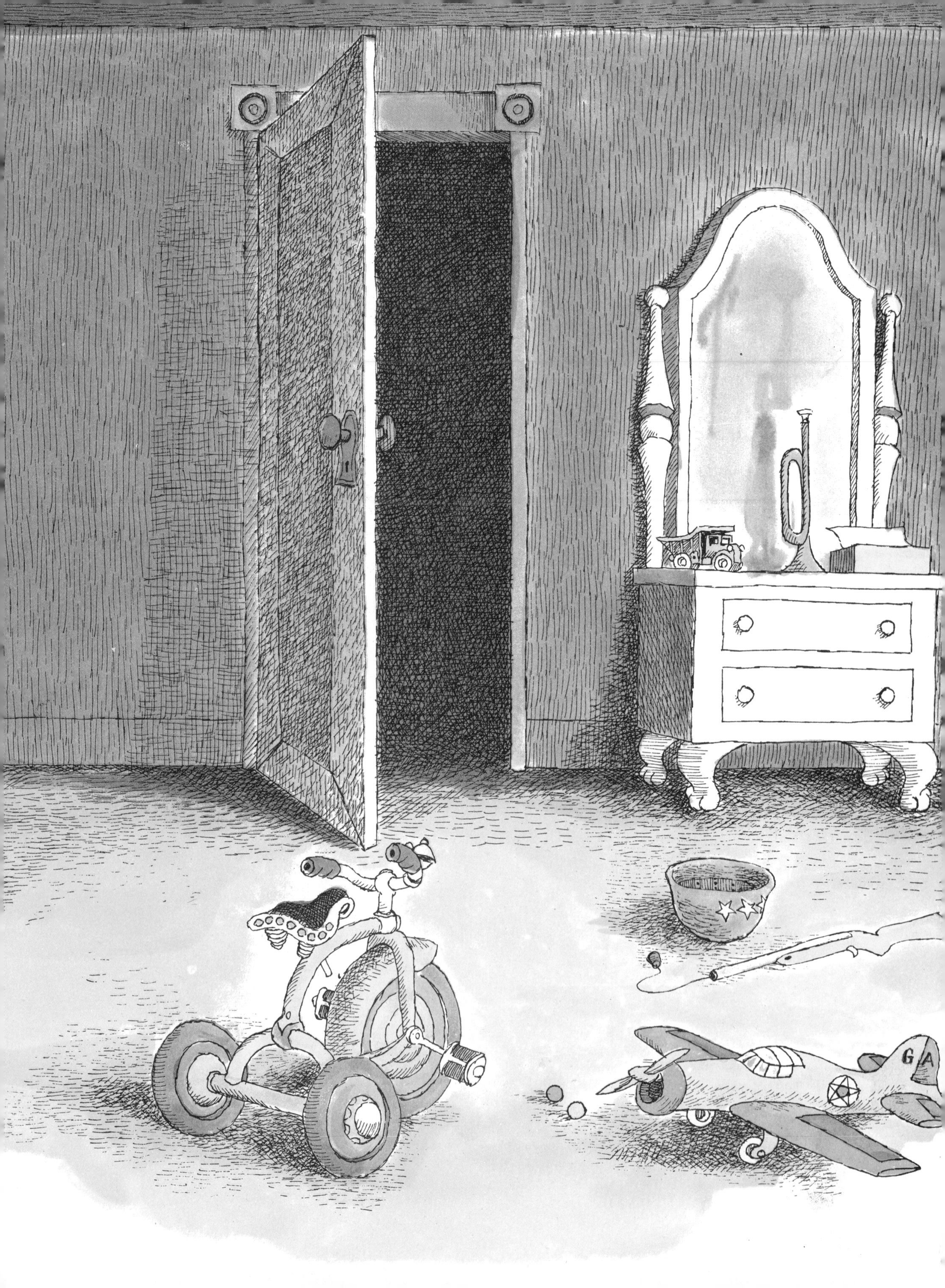
GA

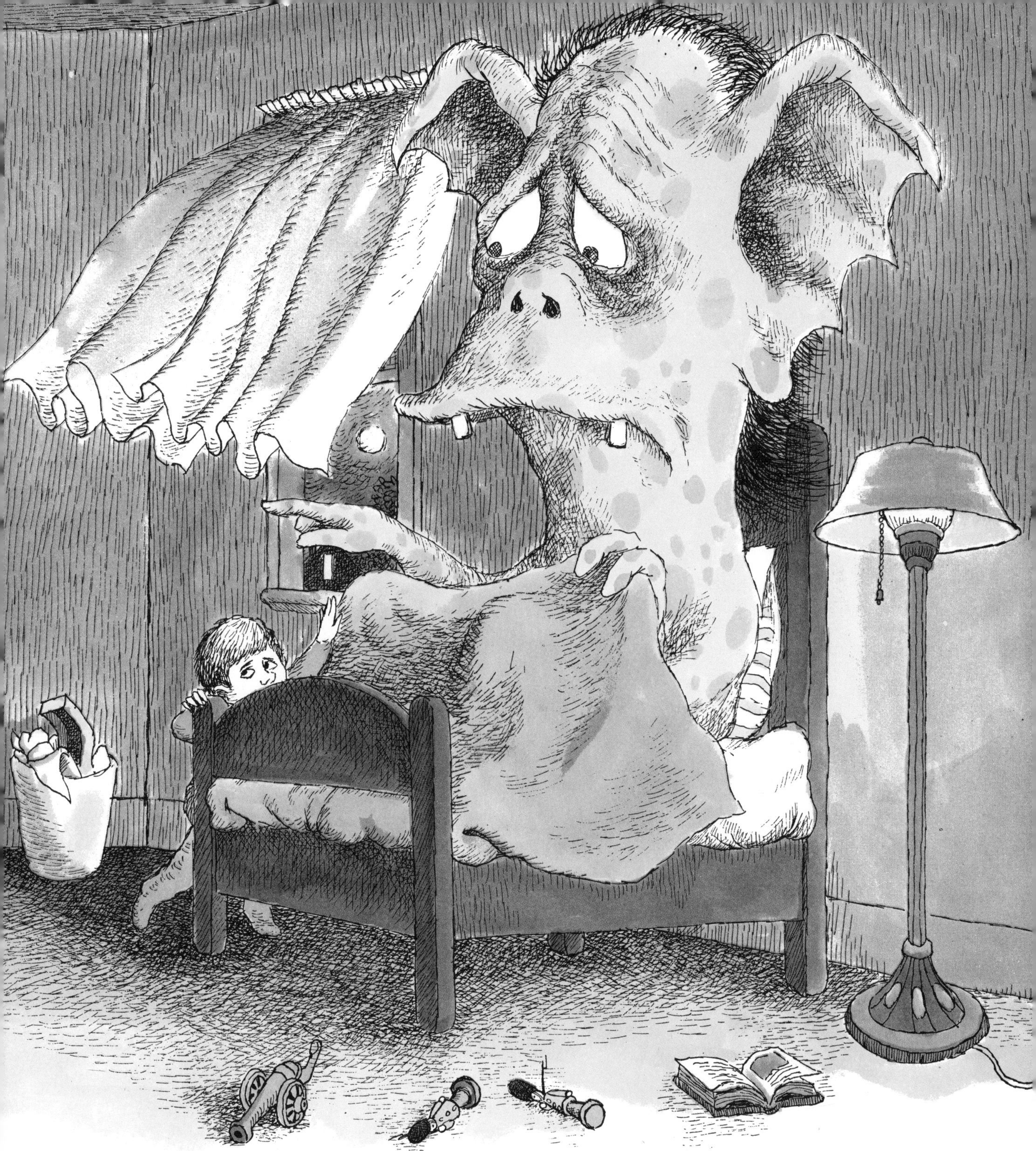

and tucked him in bed

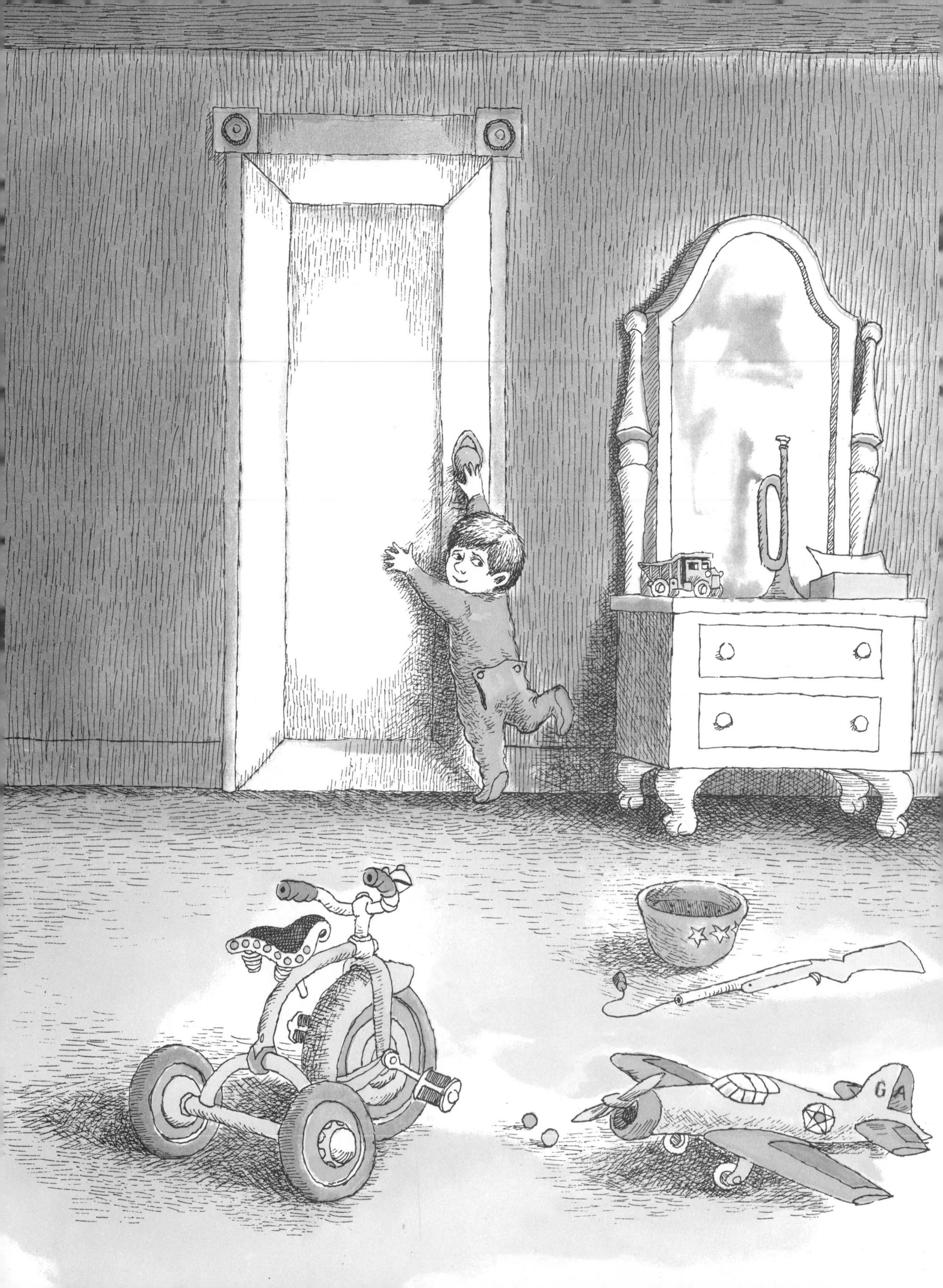
GA

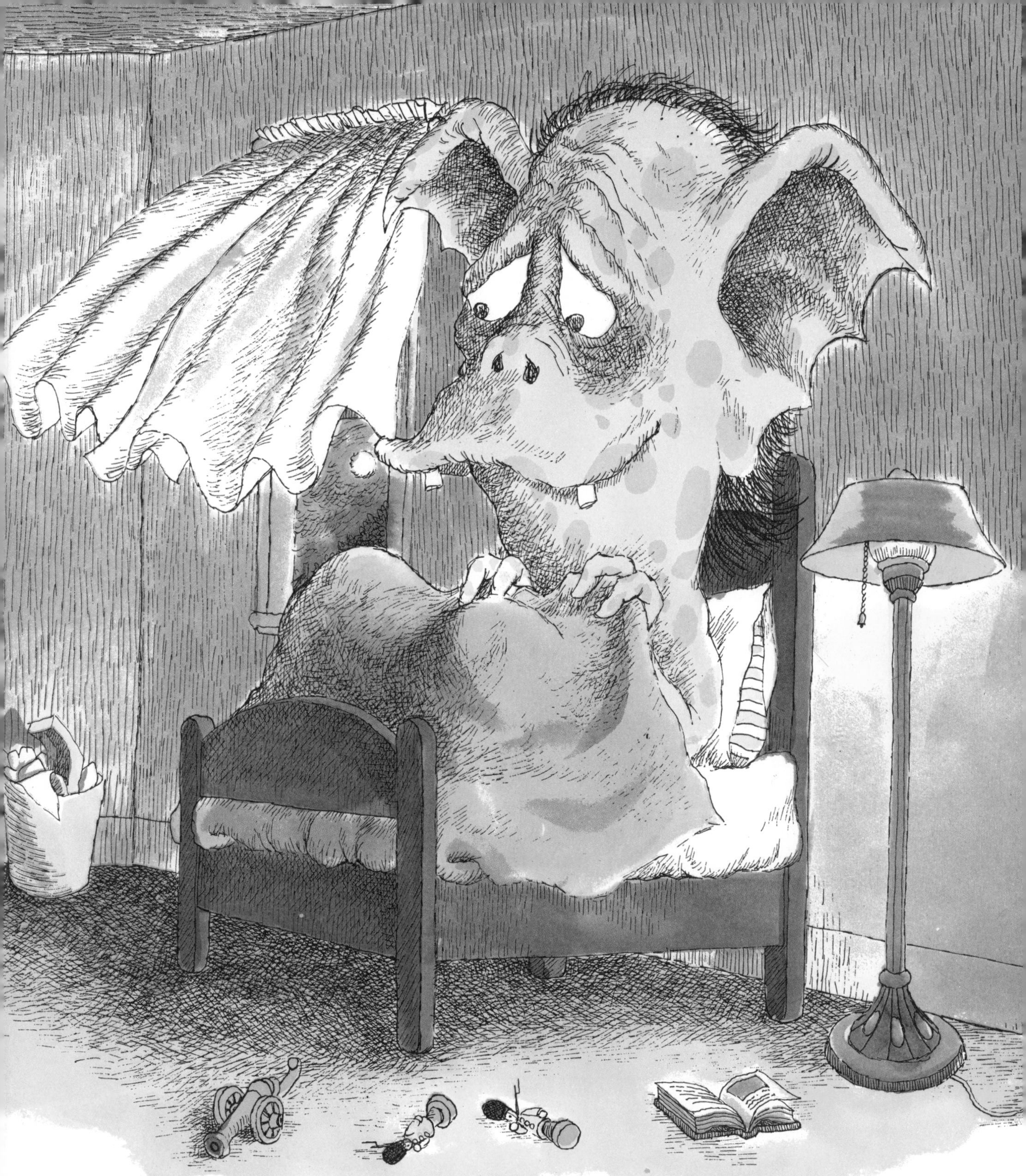

and closed the closet door.

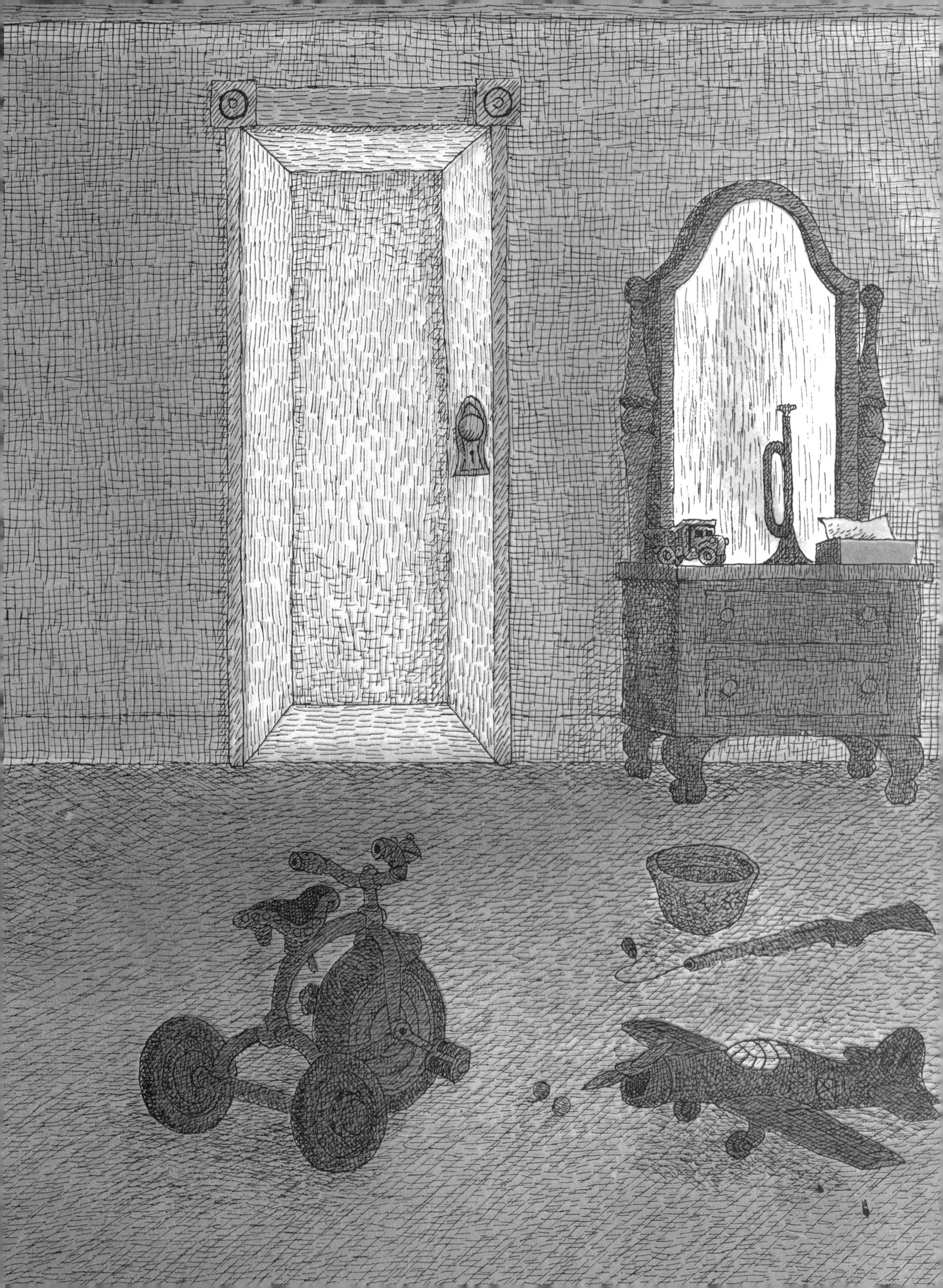

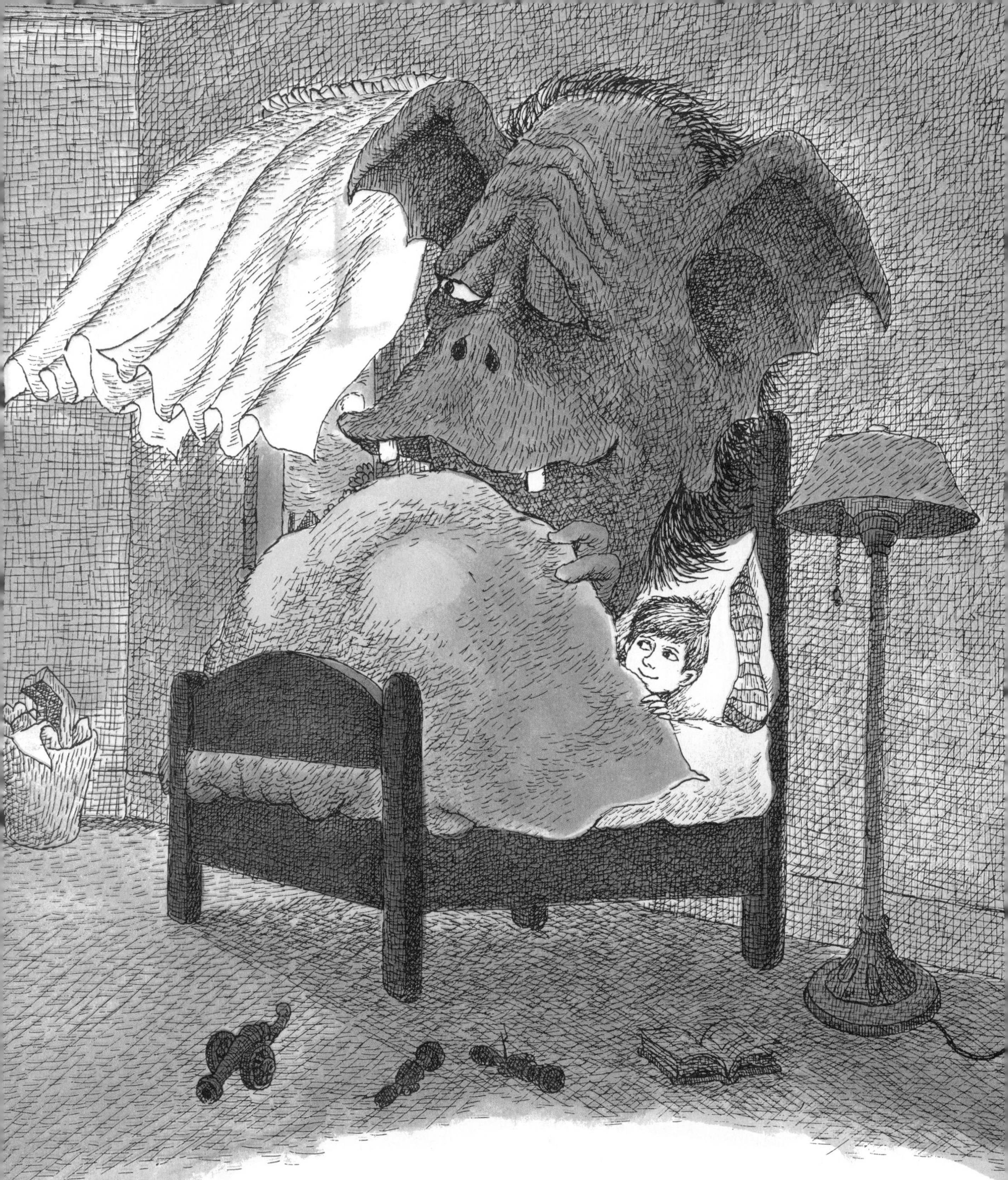

I suppose there's another nightmare in my closet, but my bed's not big enough for three.

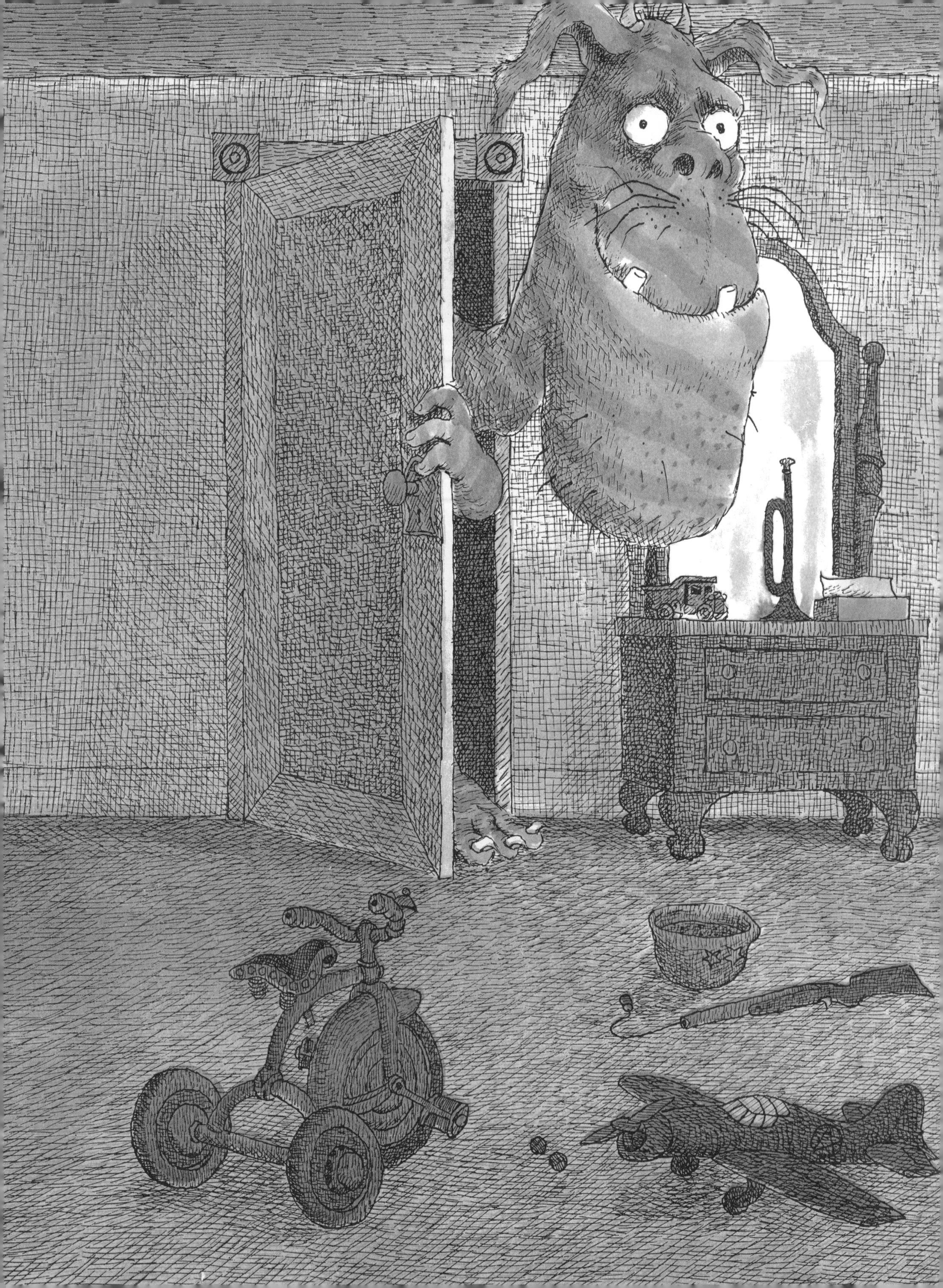

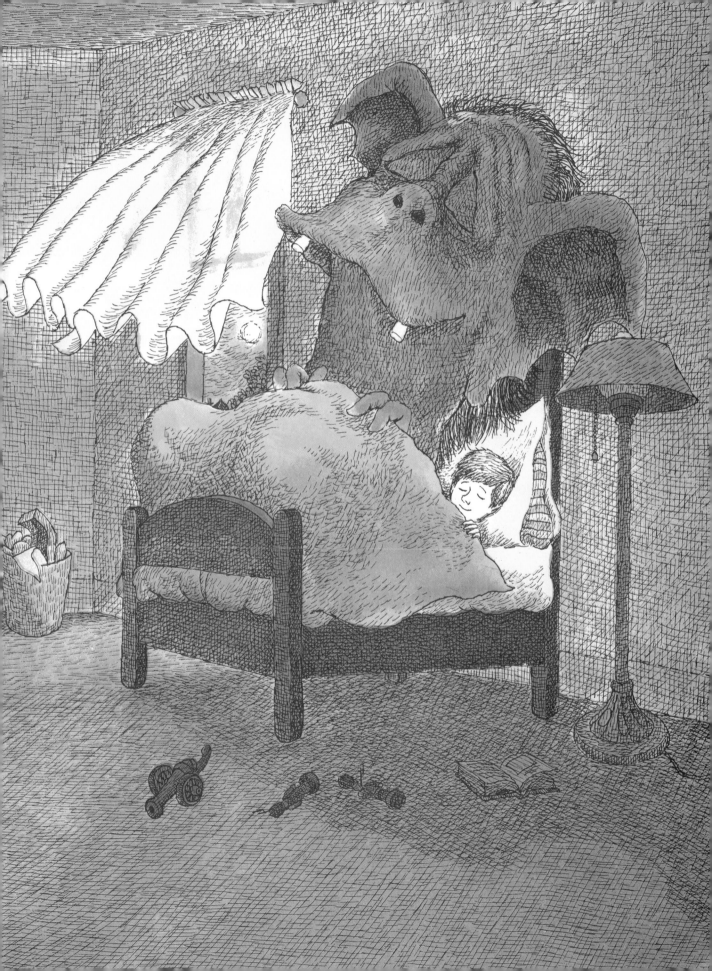